Marmalade
Hits the Big Time

"Lord Pratt and Lord Spratt," said Marmalade. "We've come for a jolly good nosh-up, and then we want a bed for the night. Big one for him, small one for me."

Other girls might not fancy trying to get into the Ritz with hardly a penny to their name. Other girls might start crying when the Doorman says, "No jeans and no donkeys!" But not Marmalade—and not Rufus either.

The worst girl in the world and her faithful (and very bad) donkey are out to hit the big time. Watch out Harrods floor managers, watch out Japanese tourists, watch out fat Greek shipping millionaires, watch out Trafalgar Square policemen, watch out Nelson's Column!

Marmalade's in town!

D1784884

Cover shows Charlotte Coleman as Marmalade Atkins in the Thames TV series Educating Marmalade produced by Sue Birtwistle and directed by Colin Bucksey and John Stroud.

Marmalade Hits the Big Time

ANDREW DAVIES

Illustrated by John Laing

A Thames/Magnet Book

Also in Thames Magnet

MARMALADE ATKINS IN SPACE
MARMALADE ATKINS' DREADFUL DEEDS
EDUCATING MARMALADE
DANGER—MARMALADE AT WORK

Magnet paperback edition
first published 1984
by Methuen Children's Books Ltd
11 New Fetter Lane, London EC4P 4EE
in association with Thames Television International Ltd
149 Tottenham Court Road, London W1P 9LL
Reprinted 1985

Published simultaneously in hardback by Blackie and Son Ltd
Text copyright © 1984 Andrew Davies
Illustrations copyright © 1984 John Laing

Printed in Great Britain by
Richard Clay (The Chaucer Press) Ltd,
Bungay, Suffolk

ISBN 0 423 01200 2

Contents

Bad Girl Warning   6

Now It Can Be Told   7

Minding Clive   9

Down and Out in the Big City   26

Marmalade and Rufus at The Ritz   37

Marmalade and Rufus See the Sights   52

Marmalade and Rufus at Harrods   70

Marmalade Hits the Big Time   81

Bad Girl Warning

If you have not read any books about Marmalade Atkins before, it is only fair to warn you that she is not a good girl. She thinks bad thoughts, she does bad things, and she Puts Herself About. She is bad enough on her own, but when she is with a certain donkey named Rufus, things tend to get *really* out of control.

Bad Donkey Warning

Rufus is in this book too.

Now It Can Be Told

Many children who have read about the Dreadful Deeds of Marmalade Atkins have asked me the same question: what happened after Marmalade and Rufus ruined the Nativity play, routed the Bulkington Silver Band, and escaped in Perkins's little grey horsebox to try their luck in the Big City?

It wasn't easy to find out. When I asked Marmalade and Rufus, Marmalade said: "That's for me to know and you to find out, cock", which wasn't much help; and Rufus closed his sleepy old eyes, shook his shaggy old ginger head, and kicked a big dent in the side of my car.

But after years of patient research I did find out in the end. It isn't a pretty story and it won't give you Nice Thoughts and Sweet Dreams, but here it is, if you really and truly want to know. Now it can be told.

Minding Clive

It all began quietly enough. A neat little grey horsebox was poozing gently along in the slow lane of the motorway heading for the Big City. In the front was a polite and boring little man called Perkins in a discreet grey uniform and a large peaked cap, humming hymns to himself as he drove. And in the back were a small girl dressed in tatty jeans and tee shirt, and a scruffy-looking ginger donkey. They weren't mucking about. They weren't doing heehaw zigzags or putting itching powder down people's trousers. They were just lolling about in the back of the horsebox minding their own business. Anyone who didn't know them would have sworn that here was a good quiet little girl and a sweet and lovable old donkey.

"This is all very well, cock," said Marmalade Atkins. "But when's the fun going to start?"

Rufus opened one eye, closed it again, and sighed wheezily. He was pretending that he was an ordinary donkey, and that he couldn't talk at all. He did it so well that Marmalade started to wonder whether he ever *had* really spoken. Perhaps she had dreamed it all: the riot at El Poko Restaurant and Nightclub, the Kenilworth Midnight Steeplechase, the whole lot. But if she had dreamed it all, what were they doing poozing down the motorway?

"Can't you go a bit faster, cock?" said Marmalade to Perkins. "I mean, they might be after us, there might be a bunch of bishops on our tail!"

Perkins took no notice at all, and Rufus gave a gentle snore.

"Well, I dunno," said Marmalade. "I thought we were going to put ourselves about a bit."

Rufus gave another gentle snore, and Marmalade realised that she was feeling quite sleepy herself. Smashing up Nativity plays and galloping through posh hotels is tiring work, and it was very warm and cosy in the little grey horsebox, warm and cosy with a comfortable smell of hay and apples and saddle soap and Rich Old Donkey. Marmalade lolled back on the cushions and felt herself drifting into a dream, in which she was in charge of an enormous brass band made up of nuns and donkeys, but the nuns wouldn't play in tune and the donkeys were rolling on their backs with their legs in the air braying at the tops of their voices: "Hee *haw* hee *haw* hee *haw* hee *haw* HEE *HAW* HEE *HAW* HEE *HAW* . . ."

Marmalade was awake. But the terrible heehawing went on. She looked out of the window. It wasn't donkeys. The little grey horsebox was surrounded by huge white police cars with red stripes down the sides, flashing their blue lights and sounding their sirens.

"Oh, no," said Marmalade. "My Dad's gone and set the police on us. He must be really cross."

"Armed police!" came a voice over a loudhailer. "Throw out your weapons and come out of the van with your hands on your heads!"

"Think I'm a bloomin' contortionist or what?" grumbled Rufus to himself.

"Oh, found your voice have you?" said Marmalade. "This is a fine mess you've got us into. S'pose we'd better do it, though, eh? Tell you what, we'll walk down the ramp quietly, then do a heehaw zigzag through the nearest hedge. OK?"

But Rufus shook his shaggy head in a weary and hopeless sort of way. He wasn't going to be any help at all.

"Throw out your weapons!" came the voice again.

"All right, cock, keep your whistle on," said Marmalade. She didn't have much in the way of weapons, but she threw out a packet of itching powder and a couple of old horseshoes.

"Ow!" said the voice on the loudhailer. "That's my big toe, if you don't mind! Now open the doors and come out slowly, and no more funny business!"

Marmalade opened the doors. She found herself staring into the startled faces of seventeen big policemen, three of whom were kneeling down pointing guns at her. There was a long silence.

"Er . . . sorry," said the senior policeman, who had a pink embarrassed face and a rather pretty black and white checked ribbon round his hat. "Wrong van."

The other policemen started to put their guns back in their holsters in a shamefaced sort of way.

"You mean you're not after us at all?" said Marmalade.

"Oh, no, miss, perish the thought! The policeman's job is all about taking *care* of little girls and donkeys, not frightening them with sirens and loudhailers. I really must apologise!"

"Yes, you really must, cock," said Marmalade, who was beginning to enjoy herself. "Come on then, get on with it."

The senior policeman cleared his throat.

"My sincere regrets on behalf of the police force for this rude interruption to your journey, miss," he said. "An unfortunate case of mistaken identity for which someone, and it'll probably be me, will get a jolly good talking to. Please accept these tokens of our good will." And reaching into his pocket he produced a large black and white checked lollipop for Marmalade, an enormous carrot for Rufus, and a signed photograph of the Chief Constable for Perkins. (Perkins looked rather glumly at his present. He would much rather have had a lollipop, or even a carrot. Life was often like that for Perkins.)

"I wonder if we can be of any assistance to you," said the senior policeman, who had recently read a book on How Not to be Beastly to the Public. "Would you like a police escort at all for the rest of your journey?"

"Well that might be rather . . ." said Marmalade, and then noticed that Rufus was shaking his shaggy head again. "I mean, no thanks cock, we prefer to keep ourselves to ourselves."

When the fleet of police cars had roared off into the distance, and the little grey horsebox was bumbling along again in the slow lane, Marmalade said to Rufus:

"What was all that fuss about then?"

"Ah," said Rufus, rubbing a hoof down the side of his nose. "I reckon that was all about the Knicker-bocker."

"What Knickerbocker?" said Marmalade.

"Pass that paper back, Perkins," said Rufus. "'Ere you are, young Marmalade, read that for yourself. I can't be doing with a lot of reading, not in vans any road, gives me the collywobbles."

The paper was called *The Sporting Life* and this is what the headlines said:

KNICKERBOCKER GLORY STILL MISSING
FEARS FOR LIFE OF DERBY WINNER
MILLION POUND RANSOM NOTE DENIED.

"I still don't get it," said Marmalade.

"Oh dear, oh dear," said Rufus. "Well, the Knick-erbocker is a young hoss. A very fast young hoss. Used to be a nice young hoss, but he got famous for running fast, and that's when his troubles started. First he wins the Derby and gets his picture in all the papers with fat ladies kissin' him, then a bunch of Dukes and Sheikhs and Earls and that pay two million pounds for him, then he gets kidnapped, and all the police are out looking for him, but I don't reckon they're going to find him."

"Knickerbocker Glory?" said Marmalade. "What a daft name for a horse."

"That's part of the trouble," said Rufus. "Give 'em a daft name, they act daft, stands to reason. All these racehorses, they all got daft names."

"Oh, yeah, right," said Marmalade, remembering Nigel's Folly and Harbottle's Revenge from the Kenilworth Midnight Steeplechase.

"Left here, Perkins," said Rufus, and the little grey horsebox rumbled down a quiet country road.

"Here," said Marmalade. "I thought we were going to London."

"We are," said Rufus. "Got a little job to do first. A minding job. Someone's got a wild young horse been kicking up rough, wants a good minder for him and no questions asked. And I'm the best minder in the business."

"*You* are?" said Marmalade.

"Everyone knows a good donkey can teach a young stallion to mind his manners," said Rufus.

"But you're not a good donkey. You're a diabolical donkey, you are," said Marmalade rather rudely.

Rufus was not offended.

"Ah, but they don't know that, do they? Now listen hard, girl, while I tell you what's what, because you'll have to do all the talking when we get there."

Marmalade listened hard and Rufus told her what was what, and the little grey horsebox rumbled and bumbled along the country road, and then a narrower country road, and then a country lane, and then a narrower country lane, and finally along a bumpy mud track so overgrown with trees and bushes that it was like driving through a haunted forest. As Marmalade looked out through the little window in the back she could see the undergrowth swishing into place behind them. She had the feeling that they were making their way to the most secret and sinister hideout in England, and she hoped very much that Rufus knew what he was doing.

Suddenly the van jerked to a halt. Marmalade stared through the windscreen. There in front of the van stood one of the biggest men she had ever seen, with the whole of his face covered in bandages. Marmalade thought he looked very much like the main character in a late night film she had seen called *The Curse of the Mummy's Tomb*, and she was glad she had Rufus's shaggy warm mane to hold on to.

"Does your Mummy know you're out, cock?" she said, trying to sound braver than she felt.

"Never mind that," said the mummy, peering through the holes in his bandages with his little bloodshot eyes. "And who would you be at all?" He had an Irish accent, which struck Marmalade as odd for a mummy—surely they were Egyptian?—and not quite so frightening.

"Marmalade's the name, and minding's the game," she said firmly.

"Ah, to be sure, and I'm glad to see you," said the huge bandaged man, lumbering stiffly over to a gate half hidden in the hedge, "for that beast has the devil in him, and he and I don't hit it off at all. Drive through now, and see for yourself."

Perkins drove the little horsebox carefully through the narrow gate into a neat little yard, with a cottage and some stables. Two of the stables were open, but the third had been newly painted and had big iron bars across the front of it, and a huge new shiny padlock the size of an alarm clock. In front of this stood a small thin man with bandy legs, a foxy face, and a checked cap pulled down over his eyes.

Marmalade opened the van door and Rufus mooched out down the ramp, yawned, and peered sleepily at the little man.

"So this is the famous minder," said the foxy little man. "He don't look much to me."

"Best in the business," said Marmalade, trying to remember what Rufus had told her. "Our terms are twenty pounds a day plus keep, good straw to sleep on, hay and apples for him, sausage and mash for me, don't worry about Perkins, he'll look after himself, and we want a week's money in advance, cock." And she held out her hand.

"Ho ho ho," said the foxy little man. "No one pulls a trick like that on Foxy Shamus Sharp. That's a bad lad we have in that stable, will you look what he was after doing to poor Pat Pratt here. Will you tell the young lady, Pat?"

"I was only giving him the time of day," said Pat Pratt mournfully through his bandages, "and he bit four of my fingers to the bone, then stood up on his hind legs and came down on me head with the front ones, turned round and kicked me through the hedge with his back ones, then he followed me through and rolled on me, he did. He's a bad lad, he is so, and he and I don't hit it off at all."

"See what you mean, cock," said Marmalade.

"So you'll understand," said Foxy Shamus Sharp. "No money in advance till we see if your donkey can do the business."

Marmalade looked at Rufus, and Rufus nodded his head very slightly.

"All right, cock," said Marmalade bravely. "Open the cage!"

They walked over to the big stable. While they were still five yards away, a shrill whinny and a snort came from inside. Marmalade peered through a crack in the door and made out the silhouette of a huge beautiful stallion with wild eyes flashing in the darkness. Then the shape became a blur as the Bad Lad bucked and reared and began trying to kick the stable to bits. The sound of it was like being in the front row of a Heavy Metal concert in the middle of a drum solo, and Marmalade put her hands over her ears.

"Are you sure you want to go through with this?" she said. Rufus nodded again, and Foxy Shamus unlocked the padlock and slid back the bars. He opened the doors and Rufus strolled in. Then the door was shut behind him.

There were five or six more loud crashes, then silence. The silence went on for a long time.

"Reckon he's done for your donkey," said Foxy Shamus. "Will you be after having a look, or will I send for the horsemeat man?"

"I'll have a look," said Marmalade, hearing her

17

voice tremble a little bit. Even the Worst Girl in the World has the odd moment of doubt, and Marmalade was beginning to think that maybe something dreadful really had happened to Rufus.

Very carefully she opened the door a little way and crept in. It was dark inside, and at first she couldn't see anything except big dark shapes. Then the shapes became clear. The tall stallion was standing quite still in the middle of the stable with his handsome head down, sweating and shivering, and Rufus was standing very close to him with his shaggy head right next to the stallion's, as if he were whispering in his ear.

"What a daft young hoss," said Rufus. "Put his head collar and bridle on, Marmalade, he won't hurt you. Call him Clive, that's his proper name."

"Come on then Clive," said Marmalade a little nervously, and the Bad Lad nuzzled her politely and stretched his neck out. As Clive stood still for his head collar to be fastened, Marmalade noticed how smooth and glossy the leather was, expensive gear, with little brass letters "KG" set into the headband. This reminded Marmalade of something, but she couldn't think what.

"Right," said Rufus. "Lead him out."

Marmalade opened the door and led Clive out into the pale sunshine. When the Bad Lad saw Pat Pratt he gave him a nasty look, but Marmalade said, "Steady on, Clive cock," and led him in a quiet circle round the yard with Rufus shambling along behind.

"Well," said Foxy Shamus Sharp. "You're a powerful good firm of minders, the pair of you, and that donkey can do the business. One week's money in advance, and no questions asked." And he held out a wad of ten-pound notes.

Marmalade and Rufus led Clive into a little paddock surrounded by high hedges and trotted him round in it, letting him stop every couple of minutes to crop the grass. Clive was not being a Bad Lad. He was being a very good lad indeed.

"But how did you *do* it?" puffed Marmalade.

"Just told him a couple of things for his own good. I used to know his Uncle Bert, I did. Now he *was* a bad lad."

Foxy Shamus Sharp and Pat Pratt leaned on the fence to watch. The pale sunlight glinted on Pat Pratt's horrible yellow Wellies, and the horseshoe pin on Foxy Shamus's horrible yellow tie which had pictures of foxes' heads all over it. Every time he went past them, Clive tossed his head and showed his teeth.

"He don't like yellow, see," said Rufus. "Never met a fast horse who did."

That night Rufus went to bed with Clive in the big stable, and Marmalade went over to the cottage and played snap with Foxy Shamus and Pat Pratt. She won every game, partly because Pat was a bit slow on the uptake and had trouble seeing through his bandages, and Foxy Shamus seemed to have his mind on other things. When Marmalade's winnings amounted to forty-three pence she said goodnight and went to her bedroom in the little hayloft over the stable. It was warm and cosy and Marmalade found herself drifting pleasantly . . .

Suddenly she was wide awake. KG! That was what

had been at the back of her mind, and now she knew what it meant! She scrambled down the ladder to the stable below and shook Rufus by his scruffy old mane.

"Rufus! Wake up, cock! I know what KG stands for! You know who Clive really is? He's the stolen racehorse! He's Knickerbocker Glory!"

As soon as she said that, Clive shuddered, jumped a foot into the air, and let fly with both hind legs at the same time, narrowly missing Marmalade's head.

"Here, leave it out, Clive cock," said Marmalade, and the stallion simmered down slowly, chuntering to himself and click-clacking his enormous teeth.

"Don't call him that, he don't like it," said Rufus.

"You mean you knew all the time?"

"I had me thoughts about it," said Rufus modestly.

"But that means Foxy and Pat are crooks! We could turn 'em over to the police! There might be a reward! We'd get our picture in the papers!"

"Don't want me picture in the papers," said Rufus grumpily. "Anyway, Clive don't want to go back to them Earls and Sheikhs, nasty jockeys riding on his back, fat ladies kissin' him and spillin' champagne down him. He likes a quiet life."

"See what you mean, cock," said Marmalade. "But look. If Foxy and Pat get their ransom, he'll go back anyway!"

"Right," said Rufus. "We better think of a plan."

"I've got a plan," said Marmalade Atkins.

Early next morning Marmalade went off on a little shopping trip to the nearest town in Perkins's van. She bought some things in a shop, then told Perkins to park the van at the end of the lane. Foxy Shamus Sharp never noticed that she had gone. He was busy with some important long-distance phone calls about Finalising the Details and Delivering the Goods and One Million Smackeroos in Used Fivers.

When Marmalade got back, she led Clive out for his morning exercise, and Foxy Shamus and Pat Pratt came out to lean on the rails.

"Change of plan," said Foxy Shamus. "This is your last day as minders. We've found a new home for the bad lad."

"Suits us, cock," said Marmalade. "We've got to be off to the Big City anyway. Come on, Rufus, let's get going!"

"No, no," said Foxy Shamus. "You have to wait till we hand the Bad Lad over and get our million . . . I mean get everything settled right and proper."

"Can't be done, cock," said Marmalade. "But I'll let you into a little Minder's Secret. Then the Bad Lad will be as good as gold for you."

"What secret?" said Foxy Shamus.

"Yellow berets," said Marmalade. "Wear a yellow beret, he'll follow you anywhere!" and out of her pocket she pulled two enormous yellow berets about the size of two big cowpats.

"You don't wear one yourself," said Foxy suspiciously.

"Don't need to, do we cock?" said Marmalade. "*We're* professional minders."

Foxy Shamus Sharp and Pat Pratt put on their

enormous yellow berets. As soon as Clive the stallion saw them, he went ape. Marmalade had not been telling a lie when she said that the Bad Lad would follow them everywhere. He did. First he jumped over the rails and followed them into the stable yard, and kicked Pat Pratt into the stable loft, then he followed Foxy Shamus Sharp into the cottage and kicked him through the roof, and then he followed them both all the way down the lane and ate their yellow berets with great enjoyment. Then he trotted back to the paddock in a very calm, peaceful and satisfied way.

It was a bit of a squash in Perkins's van as it bumbled away from the crooks' hideout.

"What are we going to do with Clive?" said Marmalade. "Is he coming to the Big City with us?"

"Not 'im, silly young hoss," said Rufus. "Only go to his head. He wants a quiet life. We'll take him down to see Perkins's Mum. That's what we'll do."

"Hope she doesn't like yellow," said Marmalade.

Perkins's Mum turned out to be a nice fat little old lady with a pink face and a pink dress and a pink cottage with pink roses growing up the walls. At the back of the cottage was a small field with purple clover and a fat grey donkey called Nellie. Clive had no objection to pink, or green or grey, or purple, and he soon made friends with Nellie, who was one of Rufus's old girlfriends.

"Brought you a pony to keep Nellie company, Mum," said Perkins.

"Looks a big pony," said Mrs Perkins doubtfully. Luckily she was a bit shortsighted. "Take a lot of hay to feed that jolly boy."

Rufus nudged Marmalade and Marmalade got out her wad of Minding Money.

"No problem, cock," said Marmalade. "The hay's on us."

"Thank you kindly," said Perkins's mum. "Would you like a cup of tea?"

Marmalade went in and had a cup of tea and about fourteen cream buns with Mrs Perkins, while Rufus went off for a rather long chat with his old girlfriend Nellie. It was getting dark by the time they left the little cottage, with Clive and Nellie looking over the fence and Perkins's mum dabbing at her eyes with a pink cotton handkerchief, and it was very dark by the time they reached the Big City.

Marmalade and Rufus stood on the Thames Embankment in the darkness watching Perkins drive slowly away in the little grey horsebox.

"Right," said Rufus. "Better find somewhere to stay. How much money we got?"

"Nothing," said Marmalade.

"What d'you mean, nothing? What about our Minding Money?"

"Gave it to Mrs Perkins, didn't I?"

"What, *all* of it?"

"Sorry, cock," said Marmalade.

"Oh, dear," said Rufus. "Oh, lor. You know what that means. We're down and out and stony broke in the Big City!"

Down and Out in the Big City

I don't know whether you have ever been to London, but if you haven't, here is a bit of advice for you. *Take some money*. If you have a lot of money, everything is fine. Bus conductors and taxi drivers let you loll about in their buses and taxis and take you wherever you want to go. Theatres and cinemas and circuses and funfairs and amusement arcades throw their doors open wide and do their best to give you a good time. Hotel owners let you sit at big tables with posh tablecloths and silver knives and forks, eating anything you like, and then they let you sleep in their beds, and they smile and bow and rush around getting anything you ask for. All you have to do with these people is *give them a lot of money*. That's all. It works like magic.

If you haven't got any money, things are quite different. They won't let you ride in their buses and taxis even though they have plenty of room. The theatres and cinemas and circuses and funfairs and amusement arcades shut their doors in your face. They don't care whether you have a good time or not.

Nobody will give you anything to eat and no one will let you sleep in their beds. It isn't very nice, but that's how it is. If you are in the Big City without any money, you have a problem, and the problem is called being Down and Out and Stony Broke.

Marmalade and Rufus were Down and Out and Stony Broke in the Big City because Marmalade had given all the Minding Money to Mrs Perkins to buy hay for Clive the racehorse. Coming to the Big City had seemed like a great adventure, but now Marmalade wished she had stayed in Mrs Perkins's pink cottage and slept in Mrs Perkins's pink soft bed, even though it had a soppy pink eiderdown with flowers on. She even had a sneaking feeling that she'd rather be at home with awful Mr and Mrs Atkins. At least it was warm in her little bedroom. It wasn't warm in the Big City; in fact it was quite chilly down on the Thames Embankment as Marmalade and Rufus leaned against the smooth stone wall looking down into the swirling black water of the River Thames. A stiff cool breeze ruffled Marmalade's tee shirt and raised goosepimples on her bare arms. She snuggled close to Rufus's scruffy ginger coat. She was thinking about Gypsy and Torchy and Rover the Free Range Piglet, and wondering what they were doing and whether they were missing her. She knew her mother and father wouldn't be missing her. They had probably forgotten all about their little girl. Sometimes it isn't easy being the Worst Girl in the World, and the truth is that just now the Worst Girl in the World was feeling sorry for herself.

"Huh! Serve her right!" I hear you saying. "She's got no one to blame but herself. She ought to be good like us, then she wouldn't get into a fix like this!" Well, all right. Fair enough. You think that if you like. But the question is, what's she going to do about it?

Rufus was not any help at all, apart from being warm to snuggle against. He just stared miserably into the dark swirling water wheezing softly to himself.

"I lived a long time, I have," he wheezed. "I known bad times, and I known good times. And this be one of the bad times." The truth was that Rufus had lived all his life in the country, and though he'd always fancied putting himself about in the Big City, he wasn't sure how to go about it.

"Come on, Rufus cock," said Marmalade. "Think of it as a challenge. How about robbing a bank?"

"All shut," said Rufus gloomily.

"Oh, yeah, right cock," said Marmalade, feeling rather relieved, as she wasn't sure how bank robberies worked. (This was long before she had met Bonzo Brown or Mean Machonochie.)

"Well how about doing a bit of mugging?" (She wasn't quite sure what mugging was either, but she had an idea that it was a quick way for bad girls to make some money.)

"We haven't got a mug," said Rufus.

"Oh, no, cock. Shame, that," said Marmalade. "Well, anyway. We're not doing ourselves any good here. Let's walk up towards the bright lights, eh?"

One small girl and one scruffy ginger donkey trudged wearily along the hard pavements and past the brightly lit shop windows of the Big City, while rich people whizzed past them in their posh cars and taxis, on their way to eat their heads off in posh restaurants and laugh their heads off in posh theatres, and none of them took any notice of Marmalade and Rufus. But all the time the lights were getting brighter and the traffic noise was getting louder and the crowds were getting thicker, and then Marmalade and Rufus turned a corner and found themselves in a big square full of big cinemas and amusement arcades. Great long queues of people were standing waiting patiently to get into the cinemas and spend their money.

And there were other people there too. They weren't rich people. They were most of them scruffy and down on their luck like Marmalade and Rufus. They stood by the queues with their hats and caps upside down on the pavement in front of them. Some of them were playing guitars and some of them were singing. Two little old men were banging spoons on their knees, and two other little old men in long black vests and toothbrush moustaches were doing wiggly dances in a big box of sand. (You may think I am making all this up, but if you ever go to London, go to Leicester Square, and you can see for yourself.)

Marmalade and Rufus watched all this with great interest. Clatter clatter went the spoons, twang twong widdly splung went the guitars, swish scratch wriggle bom swish scratch wiggle bom went the wiggly dancers. And as the queues of people shuffled along, some of them were dropping money into the upturned hats and caps.

"Here," said Marmalade. "We could do that."

"We haven't got any money," said Rufus gloomily.

"We've got a hat though," said Marmalade. "May I?" And she took off Rufus's battered straw hat and put it upside down on the pavement in front of them.

"Right," said Marmalade. "Let's put ourselves about a bit."

"Do we have to?" said Rufus. "Dead embarrassing, this is. You put yourself about if you like, Marmalade Atkins, I'll just sort of stand here."

"Oh, Rufus. Sometimes you can be a diabolically disappointing donkey!" But there was nothing to be done about it. Sometimes Rufus was in the mood, and sometimes he wasn't, and when he wasn't you just had to put up with it.

Oh, well, thought Marmalade, let's have a go anyway. She took a deep breath and started to sing, jumping up and down and beating time on Rufus's ginger backside, as he stood there pretending it all had nothing to do with him. And this is what she sang:

> "The higher up the mountain
> The greener grows the grass
> Here's a ginger donkey
> Sliding on his
> Higher up the mountain
> The louder goes the drum
> Here's a ginger donkey,
> Smack him on the
> Higher up the mountain . . ."
> (and so on, like that.)

Now you or I would have been pretty impressed with this performance, but the people in the queues had seen lots of buskers before.

"Heard it! Boring!" said the customers as they shuffled along. "We want to see the donkey dancing!"

"All right, ladies and gents," said Marmalade. "You've asked for it."

"Don't let me down, Rufus," she whispered in his ear. "All you have to do is shuffle about a bit."

She took a good handful of Rufus's shaggy ginger mane, and pulled herself up on his back.

"A four-legged friend, a four-legged friend, He'll never let you down," sang Marmalade, and Rufus shuffled wearily from foot to foot. One or two of the more soft-hearted customers said: "Oh, isn't he sweet, what a dear little donkey!" and threw some pennies in the hat. But a large party of chaps in striped scarves who had come down for a football match gathered round and started mocking Marmalade and Rufus.

"Call that dancing?" they yelled. "Seen better in the old folk's home! What about the wiggle? What about the bounce? Come on, Dobbin, let's have you!"

Now Dobbin happens to be one of the rudest things you can call a donkey. Roughly translated, it means "thick as six wooden rocking horses" and if you ever try it out on a donkey of your acquaintance, make sure you have a good stout fence between you and him, or better still don't try it out at all. When Rufus heard the football supporters calling him Dobbin, he raised his head and glared at them as if waking from a deep sleep, and began to tremble all over. Marmalade quickly slipped off his back. She had the feeling that this dance had better be a solo performance.

"OK folks," she said. "Solo Donkey Dance Routine! Pennies in the hat please!"

The Solo Donkey Dance Routine started quite slowly. Glaring at the football supporters, Rufus scraped his left forefoot on the pavement three times, then his right forefoot four times, then he wiggled his bottom and kicked his back feet out sideways. A big crowd gathered round him, and the pennies started to shower into the hat.

"Go it, Dobbin!" yelled the fattest football supporter, twirling his striped scarf in Rufus's face. Rufus grabbed the scarf in his huge yellow old teeth and did a bit of twirling himself. The football supporter did a bit of twirling too. He couldn't help it, because his neck was attached to the end of the scarf. Rufus twirled him round three times, rather like a hammer thrower, then let go of the scarf, and the football supporter sailed gracefully through the air and landed in a huge litter basket full of Coke cans and half-eaten Chinese takeaways. Everybody cheered (except the fat football supporter, who was too busy taking noodles out of his ears.) Encouraged by this, Rufus rolled over on to his back, and kicked all four legs in the air, enjoying the cool night breeze on his shaggy ginger belly. Then he began to whirl round like a top. Faster and faster he went, until he was just a grey and ginger blur. The crowd gathered closer round him, clapping in time, and more pennies showered into the hat.

"Not too close, folks, let him breathe," said Marmalade, who had a good idea what might happen next. But the excited crowd took no notice. Rufus spun round on his neck, arched his back and spun on his bottom, then suddenly went up on his hind legs and straight into a Fast Tap Routine. It was actually more of a Fast Clomp Routine, because donkeys are heavier on their feet than tap dancers; in fact they are at least three times as heavy as your fattest auntie. Now we have to remember that the crowd was standing rather close, and donkeys need a lot of space to dance in. Also, Rufus was slightly dizzy from the Fast Whirling. He didn't actually mean to tread on anybody's feet, but that was what he did. He trod on quite a lot of people's feet.

When a donkey doing a Fast Clomp Routine treads on your foot, you don't feel too much like clapping and cheering and throwing money in the hat. What you feel like doing is yowling with pain, dancing about holding your bruised toes, shouting for help, calling a taxi and heading for the nearest casualty department. And that was what people did. Marmalade found herself in the middle of a panicky stampede of people rushing in every direction, knocking each other over, dropping their hot dogs and skidding wildly about on them, every single one of them seized by a sudden need to get as far away from the dancing donkey as they could in the shortest possible time. Within two minutes Leicester Square was completely empty, except for Marmalade, who was counting the pennies in the battered straw hat, Rufus, who was standing dozily about, absent-mindedly chewing the

remains of a striped scarf, and a rather nervous young policeman, who had just come round the corner.

"Now then," said the policeman. "What's going on here?"

"Nothing at all, officer," said Marmalade politely, holding the hat behind her back.

"You haven't by any chance been busking without a licence, dancing in a wild abandoned way, performing indecent rolling and toe crushing in a public place, or throwing football supporters about?"

"Do me a favour, officer," said Marmalade demurely. "Does it seem likely to you? I mean, look at us!"

The policeman looked. What he saw was a small sleepy-looking girl and a small sleepy-looking donkey. No, it didn't seem likely to him, and in any case he wasn't quite sure of the procedure for arresting donkeys, or how to deal with them if they didn't go quietly.

"Well I'll have to ask you to move along," he said. (That was what he always said when he didn't know what else to say. You can't go wrong if you move 'em along; that was his motto, and a very good one too. He hardly ever arrested people, but he had a nice peaceful time, which is not easy if you are a policeman.)

"Certainly, officer," said Marmalade politely. "Could you direct us to the Ritz Hotel?"

"With pleasure, miss," said the policeman, impressed. "Just along Piccadilly there, you can't miss it."

"Thank you so much, officer," said Marmalade, and the two friends walked quietly off down the deserted street towards the Ritz Hotel. The policeman watched them go, wiping a sentimental tear out of the corner of his eye with his navy blue Police Issue hanky, thinking to himself what a very nice class of little girls and donkeys you sometimes met on the beat.

When Marmalade and Rufus were out of sight, all the people came running out of the doorways and cinema foyers and underground stations and public toilets where they had been hiding, and rushed up to the policeman to tell him how they had been assaulted by a mad donkey who had performed indecent rolling on them, crushed their toes, and thrown them into giant waste paper bins.

"Pull the other one," said the policeman. "I wasn't born yesterday. Come along, ladies and gents, move along, move along. I don't want to have to arrest you for being extremely silly in a public place and spreading nasty rumours about poor dumb animals, now do I? Move along please, move along."

Meanwhile, Marmalade and Rufus had arrived at the front door of the Ritz Hotel.

Marmalade and Rufus at The Ritz

The Ritz Hotel is one of the poshest hotels in London, and not used to bad girls and scruffy donkeys. The reason why Marmalade told the policeman she was going to the Ritz was that it was the only hotel in London she could remember the name of. Her father had often mentioned it. When he went down to London to sell things to Sheikhs, he often met them for tea at the Ritz. (The Sheikhs would pay the bill.) The Ritz is a very nice place to be, except when it comes to paying the bill. The cream cakes are the creamiest in the world, the steaks are the juiciest in the world, and the beds are the softest in the world. But if you ever go to the Ritz, *make sure someone else is paying the bill*.

Mr Atkins always made sure that someone else was paying the bill. On one occasion the Sheikhs didn't turn up, and after Mr Atkins had eaten sixteen cucumber sandwiches and seven cream cakes, the waiter brought him the bill. It cost so much that Mr Atkins decided he would have to do a Mad Dog. Doing a Mad Dog means running out of a restaurant very fast when they bring the bill, howling at the top of your voice. It usually works if you run fast enough, but you can only get away with it once in each place, unless you go back in disguise. Doing a Mad Dog is also against the law, and even Mr Atkins, who was a bit of a crook, would only do Mad Dogs in extreme emergencies. But he was fond of the Ritz Hotel, even though he always had to wear a false moustache when he went for tea there, and this was how Marmalade and Rufus found themselves walking up the steps to the main entrance.

At the top of the steps stood an enormous doorman in a large peaked cap and a uniform so thickly decorated with medal ribbons and festooned with gold braid he looked like a cross between a Christmas tree and the survivor of a spaghetti fight.

"Evening, cock," said Marmalade. "Don't tell me, I know—you went to a party as a Christmas tree and someone pelted you with spaghetti!"

The doorman turned crimson and his eyes bulged like lollipops. "I am the Head Doorman at the Ritz," he said, "and you are a rude little girl. The rules here are no jeans and no donkeys. Kindly leave the premises, or you'll feel the toe of my shiny black boot!"

Marmalade thought quickly. "Just my little joke, cock," she said. "And you've got it all wrong. My friend and I are eccentric millionaires, and *we've* just come back from a fancy dress party. I went as Marmalade Atkins, and my friend here went as a donkey."

"Hee haw," said Rufus affably.

The Doorman looked at them suspiciously. It didn't sound a very likely tale, but then some millionaires *are* very eccentric, and if he booted two real millionaires down the steps he might lose his job and have to hand in his lovely uniform.

"May I enquire your names?" he said.

"Certainly, cock," said Marmalade, trying to keep a straight face. "I'm Lord Pratt and he's Lord Spratt."

The Head Doorman gasped. Lords as well as millionaires! He decided to give them the benefit of the doubt.

"Please proceed to Reception, my Lords," he said, and stood aside. Marmalade and Rufus went through into the Grand Reception Hall and the Head Doorman watched them go, scratching his head and hoping he had made the right decision. Seen from the back, Lord Spratt's donkey costume was incredibly realistic.

"How can we help you?" said the Reception Clerk.

"Lord Pratt and Lord Spratt," said Marmalade. "We've come for a jolly good nosh-up, and then we want a bed for the night. Big one for him, small one for me."

"Very difficult, my lord," said the Reception Clerk. "The Ritz is chock-a-block tonight. A whole gang of millionaires just jetted in on Concorde, and we have only one suite left. But it's a very nice one, my lord."

"How much does it cost?" said Marmalade.

"Five hundred pounds a night," said the Reception Clerk. "It's very luxurious, though. We call it the Golden Fleece Suite, my lord, all the fittings are solid gold."

"Sounds all right, cock," said Marmalade. "Bit on the dear side, though. How about a little reduction, I mean if we made our own beds and that?"

"Ah, what sort of sum did you have in mind, sir?" said the Reception Clerk, fingering the carnation in his buttonhole.

Marmalade counted the pennies in the battered straw hat. "How about forty-three pence?" she said.

The Reception Clerk let out a short uneasy giggle. "My lord enjoys his little joke," he said. "Perhaps you have a credit card, sir? American Express? Diners Club?"

Marmalade searched the back pocket of her jeans.

"I've got this," she said, and pushed a grubby square of cardboard across the gleaming desk. Wrinkling his nose in distaste, the Reception Clerk picked it up between finger and thumb, and read what it said. On the front was:

LURNATROT PONY AND GYMKHANA CLUB
This is to certify that
MARMALADE ATKINS
is a member of this club

On the back it said:

This member is
EXPELLED FROM THE CLUB
and
BANNED FOR LIFE.

The Reception Clerk raised his eyes from the card and took his first really good look at Lord Pratt and

Lord Spratt. What he saw made him close the hotel register with a loud bang.

"You are not millionaires at all," he said icily. "You are simply a pair of oiks and down and outs trying to take us for a ride! Kindly leave at once!"

"Tell you what," said Marmalade. "You let us stay here and we *will* take you for a ride, how about that?"

"Out," said the Reception Clerk.

"Aw, come on, cock. You've got food and we're hungry, you've got beds and we're tired. We'd pay you back some day, honest. You wouldn't see us starve, would you?"

I suppose there *was* just a slim chance that the Reception Clerk might have chosen Marmalade and Rufus for his good deed of the year, but just at that moment Rufus, who was very peckish after his dance routine, leaned over the counter, pulled the carnation out of the Clerk's buttonhole, and ate it.

"That does it!" screamed the Reception Clerk. "Out this moment, the pair of you, or I'll call the police!"

"Keep your hair on, cock," said Marmalade. "Come, Rufus. We shall take our custom elsewhere."

Rufus was rather reluctant to go; he had enjoyed the carnation, and by the time Marmalade had got him out, he had eaten two flower arrangements, half a potted palm, and most of the gold braid off the doorman's epaulettes. The doorman did his level best to kick Marmalade and Rufus down the steps, but a doorman is not an even match for a donkey in a kicking match. The doorman had first go, but Rufus did a little sideways shuffle and the doorman's shiny black boot went through a plate glass window. Then it was Rufus's turn, and the doorman found himself whizzing round and round in the revolving doors like a spinning top.

"We'll be back!" yelled Marmalade, as they stood on the chilly dark pavement outside. She said it in a loud, bold, confident way, but really she had no idea how she could make a comeback at the Ritz Hotel, and what was more she was tired and hungry and she didn't know where to lay her head for the night.

"Oh, Rufus, cock," she said, "what are we going to do now?"

Rufus jerked his shaggy old head towards a little alley that led round the side of the Ritz Hotel.

"Round the back," he said. "Never seen a fence as didn't have no gap in it."

The back of the Ritz Hotel was quite different from the front. It was dark and dingy and cold as a medieval castle, with padlocked doors and bars over the windows. No chance at all of getting in. Marmalade saw a row of big cardboard boxes that had once held smoked salmon and caviare and other posh foods.

"Come on, Rufus," she said. "We could make ourselves a shelter out of them."

But when she lifted the flap of the first box an aggrieved voice shouted: "Find your own box, Sonny Jim! This one's mine, so it is!" Marmalade could just make out a pair of bloodshot eyes staring out of a whiskery face. The box was a tramp's bedroom. It was the same with all the boxes. All full of tramps and down-and-outs, some chewing on bones, some smoking dog ends, some snoring away like steam engines.

Marmalade and Rufus sat down on a grating, where the warm air coming up from the kitchens below could take the chill off their bottoms.

"Think we'll have to stay here all night?" said Marmalade.

"Something'll turn up, I dare say," said Rufus. "Something mostly does."

And just then, something did. The kitchen door flew open and a voice yelled up from the basement: "Two extra washers up needed in the kitchen. First two down the steps get the job!"

All the tramps and down-and-outs started clambering out of their boxes, and the reek of old smoked salmon and stale caviare filled the air. But Marmalade and Rufus had a head start on them and were down the steps and through the door in a flash.

"Two washers up reporting for duty, sir," said Marmalade. Luckily it was so steamy and smoky in the kitchen that the Head Chef didn't notice anything unusual about his two new employees.

"Lotsa work for you tonight, boys," he said. "We gotta bigga party in tonight. Aristotle Carioutabotl and all his friends just flown in onna Concorde, havea bigga banquet, see how they usea all the plates up!"

He pointed, and through the steam Marmalade could make out a giant sink in the corner with a pile of plates in it reaching to the ceiling. There were more piles of plates by the side of the sink, and gangs of waiters were crashing in through the swing doors bringing even more plates. It was a washer-up's nightmare.

"Leave it to us, cock," said Marmalade. "We'll sort it out for you!"

"Thatsa good boys," said the Head Chef. "Aprons over there, mops in the sink!"

Marmalade and Rufus got into their aprons (Marmalade's was about six sizes too big and Rufus's was about six sizes too small) and they got to work. It was a bit of a problem. The sink was so high that Marmalade could hardly see over the top of it. Rufus could, if he stood on his hind legs, but he wasn't used to holding a mop in his hooves, and tended to drop the plates on the floor. In the end, Rufus stood by the sink, and Marmalade sat on his back to wash the dishes, drying them on Rufus's apron. Rufus obligingly wiggled his backside to help with the drying, but as the apron didn't quite cover him, quite a few shaggy ginger hairs got on to the plates.

And what was worse, no matter how hard they worked, they still couldn't keep up. More and more waiters came crashing through the swing doors with more and more plates, many of them loaded with disgusting leftovers that had to be scraped into the bin. It was ten times worse than school dinners at the Convent, thought Marmalade to herself. Sister Purification and Sister Conception would have something to say if they saw all this carry on. They'd rant and shout and put themselves about all right . . . Marmalade stopped, and hit herself on the head with the mop. Of course. If *they* could put themselves about at school dinners, why shouldn't *she* put herself about in the dining room of the Ritz?

"Come on, Rufus," she said. "Let's get amongst 'em!"

"Thought you'd never say it," grunted Rufus, and with Marmalade still on his back, he charged through the swing doors, knocking over two waiters who were on their way in.

"Stop! Stop!" yelled the Head Chef. "You canta go in there!" But it was too late. They were in.

Aristotle Carioutabotl was one of the richest men in the world. He owned about forty-four oil tanker ships, and he went about doing exactly what he liked. What he liked best of all was jetting about on Concorde and holding huge banquets at posh hotels with all his not-quite-so-rich friends. He had terrible table manners. He spoke with his mouth full, he put his elbows on the table, he took food off other people's plates, he left lots of disgusting leftovers on his own plate, and he tended to throw bread rolls at the waiters. And he was doing all these things when Rufus crashed through the swing doors with Marmalade Atkins on his back, and skidded to a halt on the marble floor of the Ritz dining room.

He was so astonished at the sight of Marmalade and Rufus in their aprons and cooks' hats that he stopped throwing bread at the waiters and stared at Marmalade, licking gravy off his gold and diamond rings, unable for the moment to think what to say.

"Which one of you lot is Aristotle Carioutabotl?" said Marmalade.

"I am," said Aristotle Carioutabotl, speaking as usual with his mouth full, and spraying the nearest ten people with gravy. "What's this—the cabaret?"

Marmalade summoned up her best Sister Purification voice. "You," she said, "are a disgusting little millionaire! How dare you speak to me with your mouth full? I am not angry. I am not upset. I am just very, very disappointed. I have never seen such disgusting behaviour at school dinners, and you are all going to be very very sorry. Especially you, Aristotle Carioutabotl!"

A deep silence fell on the Ritz dining room. All the rich jet-setters held their breath and waited to see what Aristotle Carioutabotl would do to Marmalade Atkins. He was famous for his rages and his mad rampages.

But Aristotle Carioutabotl just sat and stared at Marmalade with his mouth wide open. Everyone could see the horrible half-chewed pheasant and venison and truffles and the glitter of his solid gold teeth. The manager rushed up to him anxiously: "Terribly sorry, Mr Carioutabotl. I'll have them thrown out immediately!"

Then Aristotle Carioutabotl found his voice at last. "No, no," he said indistinctly. "Let them stay. Never have I been spoken to like that since I was a little boy, and had a strict English Nanny. Oh, how she would tell me off and scold me! Oh, how I loved her! Oh, how I miss her! Nobody ever tell me off till this mad little girl in the apron, and I deserve it, I deserve it, I'm such a bad little millionaire!"

His mouth puckered and big tears rolled down his cheeks, mingling with the gravy stains.

"Never mind that," said Marmalade. "And we don't want any *soppy babies* here. Dry your eyes, get your elbows off the table, don't speak with your mouth full, and eat up properly. I want to see *clean plates!*"

"Yes Nanny, sorry Nanny," muttered Aristotle. He bowed his head, took his elbows off the table, and started to clear his plate (even the cabbage, which he hated) trying very hard not to eat with his mouth open.

"And that goes for the rest of you lot too!" said Marmalade. And all the other millionaires did the same. Some of them had had strict English nannies and some of them hadn't, but when Aristotle Carioutabotl gets his elbows off the table, *everybody* gets his elbows off the table, and when Aristotle Carioutabotl cleans his plate, *everybody* cleans his plate.

No sound could be heard in the Ritz dining room but the quiet clinking of the knives and forks and the clomping of Rufus's hooves as he and Marmalade walked between the tables inspecting.

"Right, cock," said Marmalade. "When you've eaten every scrap, you can pass the plates up quietly, take them into the kitchen and wash them up. The Head Chef will issue you with mops and aprons. And then, if you're *very* good, you *might* get some pudding!"

She paused, wondering whether she had gone too far. The millionaires stared at her in disbelief. They had never washed up in their lives, most of them.

"I say," said a fat and pink-faced millionaire sitting

just in front of Rufus. "That's not on—I mean—well we're the customers—I mean dash it, customers don't wash up!"

"They do tonight, cock," said Marmalade, and Rufus gave the pink-faced millionaire a moderate nudge on the back of his head that sent his face flying into his dinner.

"That's the way!" yelled Aristotle. "Go it, Nanny! Go it, donkey!"

"Quiet!" said Marmalade. "Little millionaires should be seen but not heard. Now, pass your plates up and into the kitchen with you!"

All the millionaires passed their plates up and trooped into the kitchen to wash up. They weren't very good at washing up, but there were a lot of them, and after a while they started to enjoy themselves, making glob-glob noises with the champagne glasses, and putting foam on their faces and pretending to be Father Christmases. The waiters and the kitchen staff quite enjoyed it as well. They came out of the kitchen and lounged about at the tables, eating strawberries and drinking champagne.

After half an hour, Aristotle Carioutabotl came out of the kitchen. "Please, Nanny," he said. "We've washed up all the plates. Is there anything else we can do?"

"Yes, cock." said Marmalade. "There's a lot of tramps in cardboard boxes out there in the cold. They haven't had a good nosh up for years. You can bring 'em in, and sit 'em down and buy 'em a big dinner, and you and your mates can serve it up!"

"Oh, Nanny! What a splendid idea!" said Aristotle Carioutabotl.

The manager threw the doors open and all the tramps shuffled in and sat down at the tables. Marmalade and Rufus sat down with them, and the millionaires scurried about serving up a gigantic banquet. Marmalade had seventeen plates of strawberries and cream at five pounds a go, and Rufus had seven nosebags full of fresh asparagus at five pounds a stick, and the tramps all got stuck in and ate their heads off. After about three hours Marmalade put down her spoon.

"Right, cock," she said. "We're full."

"Thank you, thank you," said Aristotle Carioutabotl. "This has been the most wonderful evening of my life!"

"You must be barmier than you look, cock," said Marmalade Atkins. "Manager! Bring him the bill!"

Aristotle Carioutabotl sat down at the table and the manager brought him the bill. The bill was about six yards long, it had so many items on it, and when Aristotle Carioutabotl got down to the bottom line (which is the bit you actually have to pay) he went white as a sheet. He tried turning the bill upside down, but it looked just as bad that way.

"Is anything the matter, sir?" asked the manager.

"No, no," said Aristotle Carioutabotl, in a rather panicky way. He sat there for a moment white and shaking, then an idea flashed into his mind. He looked around. Most of the tramps were asleep. The manager was busy with his calculator. The waiters were busy with the champagne. Rufus and Marmalade were leaning against each other, full as guns, and Rufus was snoring gently into his nosebag.

Aristotle Carioutabotl leapt to his feet. "Mad Dog," he shrieked, and raced for the front door yowling at the top of his voice. He was a fast little mover for a shipping millionaire, and he would have got away with it if Rufus had not suddenly woken up, heard the sound of what he took to be a heehaw zigzag, and launched into a heehaw zigzag of his own. Round the tables he went, heehawing at the top of his voice and kicking his back legs out, and he met Aristotle Carioutabotl in the doorway.

Aristotle Carioutabotl suddenly found he had to sit down on the floor, and did so. Rufus sat down too, staring at him in a mild and puzzled way.

"It's a fair cop," said the millionaire. "I'll pay. Suppose I'll have to sell one of my oil tankers."

Then the Manager and the waiters came rushing up.

"Thank you, thank you," said the Manager to Marmalade and Rufus. "The Ritz Hotel is profoundly grateful to you both. We should like to offer you a little reward of some kind."

"How about putting us up for a week or so?" said Marmalade.

"Certainly, certainly!" said the Manager.

"Free of charge?" said Marmalade.

"Of course, of course," said the Manager, rather less enthusiastically.

"Thanks a lot, cock," said Marmalade. "The Golden Fleece Suite would suit us very nicely."

Marmalade and Rufus See the Sights

Mr and Mrs Atkins were sitting up in bed having a late breakfast of hot buttered toast and Clementine Marmalade. Mr Atkins was feeling unusually contented and at peace with the world. No one had been stealing his cigars and feeding them to the goat, no one had been letting Rover the Piglet out of his pen, and for once he had not been woken at dawn by loud rock music and cries of "What's for breakfast, cock?" Mr Atkins pondered these happy thoughts as he popped a couple more slices of toast in the automatic Bedside Toaster.

"Marmalade's very quiet this morning, dear," he said after a bit.

"Atkins, you buffoon!" said his wife. "Have you not noticed? She's not here. She's disappeared. Our little girl is lorst and gorn!"

"For ever?" said Mr Atkins hopefully.

"Oh, Atkins! Ever the optimist!" said Mrs Atkins playfully, daintily removing a large piece of butter that had got stuck in her curlers.

"Lorst and gorn, eh?" said Mr Atkins. "Lorst and gorn where?"

"Who knows, Atkins? Kidnapped, perhaps. Shang-haied. Abducted. Transported. Or simply mislaid. It hardly matters, does it? The thing is, Atkins, she's not here, and we are, and that's all that matters!"

"Got a point there, Muriel," said Mr Atkins.

"That donkey's gone too."

"Oh, dear," said Marmalade's Dad. "That's a bit of a facer. I was going to sell him to some Arab gentlemen."

"Well, you'll just have to sell something else, won't you, you hopeless nitwit?"

Mr Atkins had the disloyal thought that it might be rather fun to sell Mrs Atkins to the Arabs, but he couldn't think of any Arabs who liked bad-tempered ladies who wore fur coats in bed and got butter in their curlers.

"About Marmalade," he said. "Shouldn't we sort of do something, report it to the police kind of thing?"

"You don't actually want her back, do you?"

Mr Atkins considered. "Well, maybe we shouldn't rush things," he said. "Give it a month or two, eh? If she hasn't shown up then, we might raise the alarm, eh?"

"Or not," said his wife.

"In the meantime," said Mr Atkins, "let's count our blessings and have some more toast. And then I thought we might motor down to London. Got a bit of business to do there."

"What a good idea! I'm sure I could find something to buy in Harrods!" said Mrs Atkins, already thinking of silver tin-openers and mink oven-gloves.

"Yes, I'm sure you could dear," said Mr Atkins gloomily. At this rate, he thought, he was going to have to sell Nelson's Column to the Arabs. Well, he'd done it before, and maybe he could do it again. But why? What was the point of it? Mr Atkins didn't often have a good think, what with Marmalade and escaping pigs and all that sort of thing, but he was having one now.

"Muriel," he said thoughtfully. "Do you ever think what the point of it all is? I mean, me thinking up things to sell and you thinking up things to buy? I mean, it's like a vicious circle sort of thing, innit? Why don't we just sort of lie about in bed and eat toast, eh? All come to the same thing in the end. Wouldn't it?"

Mrs Atkins gave her husband a hard look.

"Atkins," she said. "Thinking don't suit you, never did. And if everyone thought dreadful things like that the whole economy would collapse, you ask the Prime Minister. We're just doing our duty. D'you think I enjoy traipsing round Harrods thinking up new things to buy?"

"Well yes I did sort of—" began Mr Atkins.

"And you are absolutely right! Now let's get going and have some fun without having to worry about that dreadful little girl!" said Mrs Atkins.

As a matter of fact, there wasn't any need for Mr and Mrs Atkins to worry about their little girl (not that they were). Their little girl was doing all right. She was sitting up in bed in the Golden Fleece Suite of the Ritz Hotel, having just finished a breakfast of orange juice, scrambled eggs, strawberries, ice cream, and sausages. Rufus was just finishing his third nosebag full of oats. (He had very simple tastes in food.) They had had a lovely sleep in the supersoft and comfortable beds with sheets of golden silk. Actually, Rufus's bed had collapsed in the night. Even the strongest bed in the Ritz Hotel is not made to stand the weight of a fat ginger donkey. Rufus didn't mind a bit. He liked his beds collapsed. He lolled about on his collapsed bed, completely at his ease, watching Breakfast Television. A lady in a shiny green leotard was showing people how to do exercises, and he stared at this lady with great enjoyment.

"Rufus," said Marmalade. "Turn that thing off, and let's go and put ourselves about."

"Hang on a bit," said Rufus. "I like this lady."

"What d'you like about her?" said Marmalade.

"Looks like a leek. I likes leeks," said Rufus. Marmalade sighed and settled down to watching the Leek Lady hurling herself about on the screen. But quite soon she hurled herself right off the screen, and a fat man came on and started talking in a giggly way about birthdays and star signs.

"Looks like a mouldy turnip. I hates mouldy turnips," said Rufus, and turned off the television by banging the remote control switch with his left fore-foot. "Right, young Marmalade, what we going to do today?"

"Well, cock," said Marmalade. "Now we've found somewhere to stay and we're not down and out any more, how about going to See the Sights?"

Rufus rolled out of bed, shook himself vigorously

(a lot of shaggy brown hairs and bits of asparagus fell on to the golden silk carpet) and put his hat on.

"Right," he said. "I'm ready."

The first Sight that they went to see was the Tower of London. They enjoyed it very much, but were asked to leave before they had seen the Crown Jewels because Rufus ate the bobble off a Beefeater's hat.

The second sight that they went to see was St Paul's Cathedral. They enjoyed this very much too, and climbed right up the steps to the Whispering Gallery. In the Whispering Gallery Rufus absentmindedly let out a loud heehaw, and sixteen bishops went stone deaf.

The third Sight that they went to see was the Natural History Museum. They saw tiny little prehistoric horses that were no bigger than piglets, they saw a Giant Blue Whale as long as three buses suspended from the ceiling by chains (I never knew whales could fly, said Marmalade) and then they went to the Dinosaur Hall. The Diplodocus was enormous, the Archaeopterix was alarming, but right at the end of the hall was the prize exhibit—the terrifying Tyrannosaurus Rex.

When Rufus saw the Tyrannosaurus Rex, he let out a quavering heehaw and started backing out of the hall. Deep down, he was only a simple country donkey, and the model *was* very realistic, and seemed to be looking right at him, as if a ginger donkey was just the sort of snack he fancied.

"Come on, Rufus, cock," said Marmalade. "He's only a model, honest! Come on, I'll show you!"

Rufus was very reluctant to go any closer, but let himself be persuaded in the end.

"There you are," said Marmalade, tapping Rex's hide. "He's hollow!"

Rufus worked up a bit of courage and gave Rex a quick kick, getting ready to run away if the fearsome beast gave chase. But nothing happened, except that a few flakes of shiny brown plaster fell on the floor.

"Ah" said Rufus, relieved. "I was only 'aving you on, Marmalade Atkins. Donkeys ain't scared of dinosaurs. Still—better go now, eh?"

"No, hang on, look at this!" said Marmalade. "There's a little door in his backside! Let's go in!"

She opened the door and shone her bad girl's torch around. Inside the Tyrannosaurus Rex it was like a giant cave, and there were wooden steps leading right up to the inside of its head. Right at the top, there were two tiny points of light.

"Let's have a look, cock!" said Marmalade, and led the reluctant donkey up the steps, right to the very top.

Just as Marmalade and Rufus reached the top of the steps, they heard footsteps coming into the Dinosaur Hall.

"Better 'op it," said Rufus.

"NO, too late!" said Marmalade. "Just keep quiet."

The footsteps belonged to a party of schoolchildren, who were on a School Trip with their Headmaster, Mr Harris, and they gasped with wonder when they came into the Dinosaur Hall.

"Cor, look at that Tyrannosaurus!" said Oninka. "Isn't he big!"

"Think he's going to eat you, Oninka!" said Hon Wai.

"Think he's going to eat Mr Harris!" said Darnell.

"Now, now, children, no need to be silly," said Mr Harris. "This is, of course, just a replica or model. Now listen carefully: Tyrannosaurus Rex was the largest flesh-eating, or carnivorous creature, that ever lived on earth. Specimens have been found—"

"His eyes are moving!" yelled Pritti.

"Don't be silly, Pritti. Specimens have been—"

"They *are* moving!" yelled all the children. Mr Harris looked up at Tyrannosaurus Rex. Its eyes *were* moving, and just now they were looking straight at Mr Harris.

Mr Harris was a very brave and sensible headmaster, but even the bravest and most sensible headmasters can sometimes feel a little bit frightened.

"Line up in twos, boys and girls," said Mr Harris, in what he hoped was a calm voice. "That concludes our visit to the Dinosaur Hall. Lead out quietly."

As they reached the doorway, Mr Harris glanced back over his shoulder. The eyes were *still* looking at him. And then suddenly the giant dinosaur let out a huge roar. Well: not exactly a roar. It sounded more like the braying of a giant donkey magnified by four echo chambers and a battery of loudspeakers, and it was too much even for brave Mr Harris to take. He led the rush to the coach.

"Full speed to Sudbury, driver!" he yelled, and he

didn't stop shaking and trembling until he was safe back in his office with a nice hot cup of tea.

While all this was going on at the Natural History Museum, Mr Atkins was doing a bit of business near Buckingham Palace with a group of Japanese businessmen in black coats, striped trousers, umbrellas and bowler hats.

"Gather round, gents," he said. "Now this is very hush-hush, very confidential. Her Majesty doesn't want any publicity."

"Her Majesty, ah so," said the Japanese businessmen, nodding wisely.

"I happen to be her agent, see, 'cos she doesn't like to do business in person, right?" said Mr Atkins, and turning back the lapel of his jacket, he showed them his Official Royal Badge, which he had made the previous evening from a twenty pence piece.

"Now the thing is, Her Majesty's a bit short of the readies just at the moment. Times are hard, and those Corgis cost a fortune in Kennomeat, nothing but the best for them. Nasty little things in my opinion, but everyone to her taste, eh? Well, Her Majesty thought she might let off a few rooms to lodgers, if she could find the right sort of clients. Nice quiet people she wants, no dogs cats or parrots, no late night parties, no posters on the wall, no caravans in the front garden, if there's one thing she can't stand it's a caravan. Are you with me gents?"

"All this is perfectly satisfactory," said the senior

Japanese businessman. "Ah, which rooms does your client wish to let?"

"Whole West Wing, squire," said Mr Atkins, gesturing grandly towards the West Wing with its rows of glittering windows. The Japanese businessmen stared at the West Wing of Buckingham Palace, very impressed indeed, but trying not to show it too much.

"And the rent?" said the senior Japanese businessman.

"Five thousand nicker a week, payable in advance, Squire," said Mr Atkins, "and for that she'll throw in a free garden party every Thursday, weather permitting, and all the strawberries and cream you can eat. That's the offer. Take it or leave it, gents."

The Japanese businessmen went into a huddle while Mr Atkins looked anxiously round for policemen. Then the senior businessman bowed to Mr Atkins.

"We'll take it," he said.

"You won't regret it," said Mr Atkins. "Right, I'll just take the first week's rent now, and then we'll go in and meet Her Majesty, she can't bear to see money changing hands. 'You deal with the money side of things, Atkins,' she said to me, 'I'm far too busy ruling the country and besides I've got to bath the Corgis this morning.' Very busy woman, Her Majesty is."

The Japanese businessmen got out their wallets and handed over a big bundle of notes to Mr Atkins.

"Thank you gents," he said. "I won't count it, because I trust you, I can tell an honest face. Now if you'd like to go in and inspect the premises . . . just up this path here. And if you see one of the Royals, bow very low and don't get up till you're told . . . blow me down, there's the Duke of Edinburgh! Bow down, gents, bow down, and don't get up till the Duke gives the word!"

The Japanese businessmen bowed low, and Mr Atkins hailed a passing taxi.

"Trafalgar Square, driver!" he cried. "Got a bit of business to transact!"

"Where shall we go now?" said Marmalade to Rufus as they walked down the steps of the Natural History Museum.

"I fancies going to find a nice field and eating a bit of grass, meself," said Rufus.

"Oh, Rufus, you can do that any time!" said Marmalade.

"Well I don't want nothing too exciting," said Rufus. "We put ourselves about enough for one morning. I wants something quiet and peaceful."

"I know," said Marmalade. "We'll go and feed the pigeons in Trafalgar Square. That'll be nice and peaceful."

Quite a crowd had gathered round the Japanese businessmen as they crouched, bent over double, facing the West Wing of Buckingham Palace. Even though the crowd were making quite a lot of comments such as "Bottoms up, lads!" the Japanese businessmen didn't move a muscle because they were waiting for the Duke of Edinburgh to give them the word. After a while a policeman strolled along. It happened to be the same policeman who had moved Marmalade and Rufus along from Leicester Square.

"Now, now, what's all this?" he said. "Up you come, gents, no bending allowed at Buckingham Palace!"

The Japanese straightened up and stared at the policeman in a disappointed way.

"Where is the Duke of Edinburgh please?" said the senior Japanese businessman.

"Up in Scotland, shooting grouse, now move along please, move along."

"But we live here!"

"Ho ho ho, jolly Japanese joke, pull the other one, wasn't born yesterday, now move along or I'll have to take you in," said the policeman.

The Japanese businessmen stared at each other in horror as the awful truth dawned on them. They had been duped by a master criminal!

"Revenge! Revenge!" they cried, and running past the puzzled policeman, they hailed three taxis and set off for Trafalgar Square.

Marmalade and Rufus had a nice quiet peaceful time feeding the pigeons in Trafalgar Square. They also made themselves a bit of pocket money, because lots of tourists wanted to be photographed with Rufus at ten pence a go. Then Marmalade noticed a small group of people talking earnestly on the steps of Nelson's column. Six of the people were Arab Sheikhs in long white robes, and the seventh was a short stout man in a pork pie hat.

"He looks a bit familiar," said Marmalade to Rufus. "Let's go a bit closer and have a look."

"This is a once in a lifetime opportunity, squire," Mr Atkins was saying to the senior Sheikh. "Just think of it, your very own Nelson's Column in the middle of the desert sands, you'd be the envy of all Arabia!"

The Sheikhs nodded wisely.

"How is it that the Column is for sale, honoured friend?" asked the senior Sheikh.

"Well, you see, Squire, it's like this. The country's a bit short of cash, to be frank with you, and the Queen and the Prime Minister put their heads together and decided to sell off a few unwanted articles surplus to requirements, and jolly old Nelson's Column came top of the list. Put me in charge of negotiations, all above board, here's my official badge, now you see it now you don't. Think they're going to build a multi-storey car park here, but that's no skin off your nose. Do you want it or not, gents?"

The Sheikhs went into a huddle for a few minutes.

"How will you transport it, honourable friend?"

"Oh, dear, oh dear, transport's no problem!" laughed Mr Atkins. (Here he was telling the truth, because he had no intention of transporting Nelson's Column anywhere.) "Oh dear no, if you've got the cash we have the technology, we'll float the old boy down the Thames on an oil tanker I expect. Well, there you are gents: fifty thousand nicker to you, take it or leave it!"

The Sheikhs went into another huddle.

"Thirty thousand nicker and three hundred camels?" said the senior Sheikh.

"You drive a hard bargain, Squire, but because I like your honest faces—done! Cash in advance, gents. I'll trust you for the camels."

"No, honourable friend. Cash on delivery."

Mr Atkins thought quickly. These Sheikhs were a cunning lot. They probably didn't intend to pay at all. Downright dishonest. (Mr Atkins had forgotten for the moment that he wasn't going to deliver either.)

"Tell you what," he said. "Just so I don't get in trouble with Her Majesty—ten per cent now and we'll take the rest in instalments, I can't say fairer than that."

The Sheikhs went into yet another huddle.

"This man is either a fool or a rogue," said a thin Sheikh. "And I think he's a rogue."

"I think he's a fool," said a fat Sheikh.

"Let us take a gamble, my friends," said the senior Sheikh. "After all, five thousand is peanuts to the likes of us!"

They all got their wallets out and passed a large bundle of notes to Mr Atkins. Just as the money was changing hands, three taxis squealed to a halt, and twelve Japanese businessmen came rushing out of them. Some of them were waving umbrellas, and two of them were brandishing Samurai swords, and they were all makinig straight for Mr Atkins.

Mr Atkins looked this way and that. The Japanese businessmen were between him and the buses, and the

Sheikhs were between him and the Underground station.

"Quick, Dad!" yelled Marmalade. "Up the column!"

Nelson's Column is reckoned to be one of the hardest things to climb in the world. Many have tried and failed, but it is amazing what you can do if you have a gang of enraged Japanese businessmen with Samurai swords after you. Mr Atkins went up the Column like a grey squrrel. A rather fat grey squirrel in a pork pie hat, I admit, but up it he went in thirty seconds flat, and stood at the top of the Column with his arms round Admiral Nelson's neck and a pigeon on his head, trying not to look down.

Down below, Marmalade climbed on to a stone lion and addressed the crowd.

"Ladies and gentlemen!" she said. "Yet another death-defying feat by the Amazing Atkins! Please put your contributions in the hat provided!"

Rufus went round with his hat between his teeth and all the tourists put money into it. Soon a televison crew and three fire engines arrived in Trafalgar Square. The Japanese businessmen ground their teeth in rage because now they wouldn't be able to get at Mr Atkins. The best that they could hope for was that he would fall off.

The firemen put their longest ladder up against the column but it didn't reach anywhere near the top. Mr Atkins was beginning to panic as more and more pigeons crowded on top of his head, glad of the change from Nelson's hat, which they found rather

Marmalade and Rufus strolled over and watched them loading her Dad into the ambulance.

"Oh, er, Marmalade," said Mr Atkins faintly. "If you're not too busy, you might pop over to Harrods. Told your Mum I'd meet her there at five o'clock. If you see her, tell her I've been called away unexpected sort of thing. You might say it's been an up and down sort of day, but I did manage to do a bit of business."

Marmalade and Rufus at Harrods

Mrs Atkins was having a nice day out doing a bit of shopping in Harrods. If you don't know what Harrods is, I had better tell you that it is about the biggest and poshest shop in London. You can buy just about anything there, from a packet of peanuts to an African elephant, and if they haven't got it in stock they can get it for you. (To be perfectly honest, last time I went they were right out of African elephants, but they were tremendously polite and apologetic about it, and delivered one in a smart green van the very next day.) It really is a marvellous place, and the only snag about it is that things cost a lot of money there.

Mrs Atkins didn't mind one bit about things costing a lot of money there. That was one of the things she liked best about it. Mr Atkins was good at making money, and Mrs Atkins was good at spending it. She was brilliant at thinking up new expensive things to buy, things that you or I would never think of, such as diamond-studded dishmops and solid gold toilet seats. It didn't worry her that the diamond-studded dishmop scratched the plates, and that the solid gold toilet seat was much harder and colder to sit on than the ordinary sort; what she liked was seeing the look of rage and envy on the faces of her friends from the bridge club when they came round to see her new things and the look of horror on Mr Atkins's face when he saw the bills.

As she lived a long way from London, Mrs Atkins usually ordered things by telephone, but she liked it much better when she could actually come up to London and be objectionable in person. Mr Prettiman did not feel like this. Mr Prettiman was the Chief Floorwalker of Harrods, and had several medals for politeness and patience. He didn't much like taking Mrs Atkins's orders on the telephone, because she always gave him a headache, a sore ear, and a very sad feeling about life in general. But at least on the telephone he could make faces, hold the receiver at arm's length, and mouth "silly old bat" into his handmirror. When she was actually in his shop, large as life, he couldn't do any of these things. He had to smile and bow the whole time, because at Harrods the Customer is Always Right.

Mrs Atkins dragged Mr Prettiman through the China Department, where she bought two new gold-rimmed tea-sets and made two assistants cry, then she dragged him down to the Food Hall and stocked up on caviare and quail's eggs and smoked salmon (and a small pork pie for Mr Atkins). Then she gave the Luxury Chocolate Display a frightful hammering, taking one or two chocolates from each beautifully arranged assortment, chomping them up, and throwing the rest aside.

"Not *quite* what I wanted," she said each time. "Ah! These ones here in gold paper look promising. Is this *real* gold paper, Mr Prettiman?"

"Of course, Madam," said Mr Prettiman, smiling and bowing.

"*Solid* gold?"

"Well, Madam, I'm not quite sure. Er . . ."

"Not quite sure? Don't you know what you've got in your shop, Prettiman? Can't you answer a simple question? You're a total waste of space, Prettiman, that's what you are."

"Yes, indeed, Madam," said Mr Prettiman, smiling and bowing. "How well Madam puts it. A total waste of space, that's what I am!"

"Well no need to look so happy about it, you buffoon!" shrieked Mrs Atkins. "Oh, tell them to wrap up six boxes of whatever's most expensive, and be quick about it, I haven't got all day, I haven't even been to the Fur Department yet!"

Mr Prettiman sighed.

"Was that a sigh, Prettiman?"

"Oh, no, Madam. Well, perhaps just a tiny one."

"Aren't you enjoying yourself, Prettiman? Don't you like your work? Shall I tell them to give you the sack?"

"Oh, Madam, I'm having the most marvellous time, thank you so much for asking," said Mr Prettiman, smiling and bowing. "My greatest pleasure is to serve you, Madam."

(There's no need to feel *too* sorry for Mr Prettiman. Harrods paid him a great deal of money for putting up with the likes of Mrs Atkins).

"Well, stop going up and down like a Japanese yo-yo and conduct me to the Fur Department!" said Mrs Atkins. And off to the Fur Department they went, pausing only at the Perfume Counter, where Mrs Atkins tried out about a dozen bottles, spraying the scent about all over herself and Mr Prettiman until they both smelt like a cross between Kew Gardens and a chemistry lab.

Now if it's all the same to you, we'll leave Mrs Atkins to get on with it in the Fur Department; we all know how keen on fur she was, but I expect you agree with me that wearing dead animals is not a very nice thing to do, and that fur coats look a great deal better on their original owners.

Marmalade and Rufus had strolled down from Trafalgar Square after watching the ambulance cart Mr Atkins off to the casualty department at Charing Cross Hospital. They were both rather tired after their day of sightseeing, but they thought it only fair to deliver Mr Atkins's message after he had been so brave and entertaining, and besides, neither of them had ever visited Harrods before.

At first, they were curiously reluctant to let Marmalade and Rufus into Harrods at all, but Marmalade explained that she was Rich Miss Atkins from Warwickshire and that she was returning Rufus as Faulty Goods.

"Oh, dear, oh dear," said the Deputy Head Floor-walker, who was called Mr Smiley. "I *am* sorry to hear that, we've never had complaints about our donkeys before. Er . . . what seems to be the problem?"

"He nudges people," said Marmalade.

"Well, Madam, donkeys do nudge a little, I understand. Most people enjoy it. What a sweet little chap. Hello, there, Dobbin!"

And Mr Smiley chucked Rufus under the chin and stroked his nose. Rufus stared at him thoughtfully and gave him a nudge, and Mr Smiley staggered backwards.

"Yes, I see, he does have rather a *firm* nudge but many people nowadays . . ."

Rufus gave him another nudge, and Mr Smiley fell over. Rufus stared around vaguely as if wondering where Mr Smiley had gone, then put his front hooves on Mr Smiley's chest.

"Ah, yes, Madam," gasped Mr Smiley, doing his level best to keep smiling despite the pain in his chest. "This donkey is slightly imperfect."

"He's diabolical," said Marmalade.

"Madam puts it very well. I, er, think this is a matter for the Complaints Department on the Fifth Floor. Would you like me to accompany you?"

"It's all right, cock," said Marmalade. "We'll find our own way."

That's a relief, thought Mr Smiley, as Rufus got off his chest, leaving a muddy hoofprint. That donkey has *very serious problems*.

Marmalade and Rufus didn't go to the Complaints

Department. Marmalade had no complaints about Rufus: she liked it when he nudged people. Anyway, she had to look for her mother.

It was easier to see where Mrs Atkins had been than where she was now. In the China Department, the Food Hall and the Perfume Counter, the assistants were lying about exhausted and tearful and vowing that if they ever met anyone like Mrs Atkins again they would jump screaming out of the windows.

"Yeah, that sounds like my Mum, cock," said Marmalade cheerfully. "A lot of people feel like that about her. Still, she's the only mum I've got. Any idea where she is now?"

"We don't know, Madam, and we don't care," said the perfume assistants, smiling and bowing.

"Know how you feel, cock," said Marmalade. "Never mind, eh? Come on, Rufus."

Rufus lumbered off, leaving a powerful smell of Rich Old Donkey in the Perfume Department, and they went off to inspect some of the more interesting bits of Harrods. (Actually Marmalade had a pretty good idea that her mother might be in the Fur Department, but she didn't like to go there with Rufus. Rufus was a diabolical donkey, but he did have his sensitive side, and the idea of fur coats upset him more than somewhat. He had even heard once of something called a donkey jacket, and the mere mention of it had given him a fit of the heehaw zigzags.)

So Marmalade took Rufus with her to the Toy Department, where she had a good time winding up forty-seven clockwork ducks. The clockwork ducks in Harrods have the very best clockwork motors in them, and the ducks went waddling off all over Harrods, upsetting the customers in the tea room and frightening several fat ladies who were trying things on in the Lingerie Department.

Then they went to the Sports Department, where both Marmalade and Rufus tried on skiing outfits. Marmalade thought Rufus looked very handsome in his ski goggles and bobble hat, but his skiis didn't fit very well, and he split all the ski jackets and trousers he tried on, even the ones marked Large and Portly. He couldn't see very well out of the goggles either. When the assistants, bowing and smiling, asked him very politely to leave, he turned the wrong way and skied down an UP escalator.

When he finally came to a halt, he was feeling quite shaken up, and so were the people who had been going up the escalator at the time, and also the manager of the Glassware Department, which was where Rufus completed his descent.

"You ought to be more careful, cock," said Marmalade to the manager of the Glassware Department. "Fancy leaving a lot of glass vases in the middle of a ski run! Someone could have a nasty accident! Come, Rufus!"

What they both needed now was a rest, and Marmalade took Rufus up in the lift to the Bed Department. It was lovely and calm and peaceful in the Bed Department. Just acres and acres of beautiful big beds: low beds, high beds, feather beds, foam beds, water beds, electric vibrating beds, four posters, the lot. Best of all, there were no assistants about. Marmalade and Rufus decided to test out some of the beds. They all felt pretty good to Marmalade, but Rufus took a little time before he was suited: most of the beds were too small, and some of them collapsed as soon as he sat on them, but in the end he found one he liked: The Harrods Superstrength Reinforced Four-Poster, in Solid Oak with Solid Gold Knobs On, a very popular model with extra fat millionaires. Marmalade and Rufus only meant to test the beds out, and perhaps just have a very short rest, but they were both really tired after their busy day, and within five minutes they were both sound asleep.

Mr Prettiman, the Head Floorwalker, was feeling in need of a rest as well. He had bowed and smiled his way through all the departments of Harrods with Mrs Atkins, and was bent double under the weight of all the gold, silver and diamond articles she had bought. Mrs Atkins was well loaded too. She was now wearing four fur coats, including the one she had come in, two mink hats, and a particularly nasty and dangerous looking diamond tiara on top. But she was stronger than she looked, and certainly stronger than Mr Prettiman.

"Now," she said. "What's next, Prettiman?"

"Madam," said Prettiman, bowing and smiling, though his back ached and his face felt as though it would split, "I fear it's almost closing time, and Madam has seen everything now."

"Everything?"

"Well," admitted Mr Prettiman. "Everything except the Bed Department."

Mrs Atkins didn't need a bed, of course, but she so enjoyed tormenting Mr Prettiman, and who knows, maybe she might see something in the bed department that would take her fancy and cost Mr Atkins a lot of money, so up to the Bed Department they went.

It was quite some time since Mr Prettiman had been in the Bed Department, and he found it not quite as he expected. Some of the beds were broken, and others were covered in muddy marks and ginger hairs.

"Call this a Bed Department?" said Mrs Atkins. "It's a shambles! It's a dog's breakfast!"

"We're, er, trying for the lived-in look," stammered Mr Prettiman.

"Ha! More like the died-in look if you ask me!" shrieked Mrs Atkins, laughing at her own joke, and poking Mr Prettiman in the ribs with her new gold-knobbed umbrella.

"The, ah, the Special Editions are up at the far end, Madam," groaned Mr Prettiman. "Madam might possibly find our Superstrength Reinforced Four-Poster rather amusing."

Mrs Atkins stared at the Superstrength Reinforced Four-Poster for quite some time, her eyes bulging.

"It's got a donkey in it," she said at last.

"No it hasn't—ah, yes! Ah . . . um . . ." said Mr Prettiman desperately ". . . it's our new concept! Bed-room Sculpture! For the lady who has everything! Your very own Life-Size Donkeyform Bedwarmer! This one's just a sample, of course, you can have the

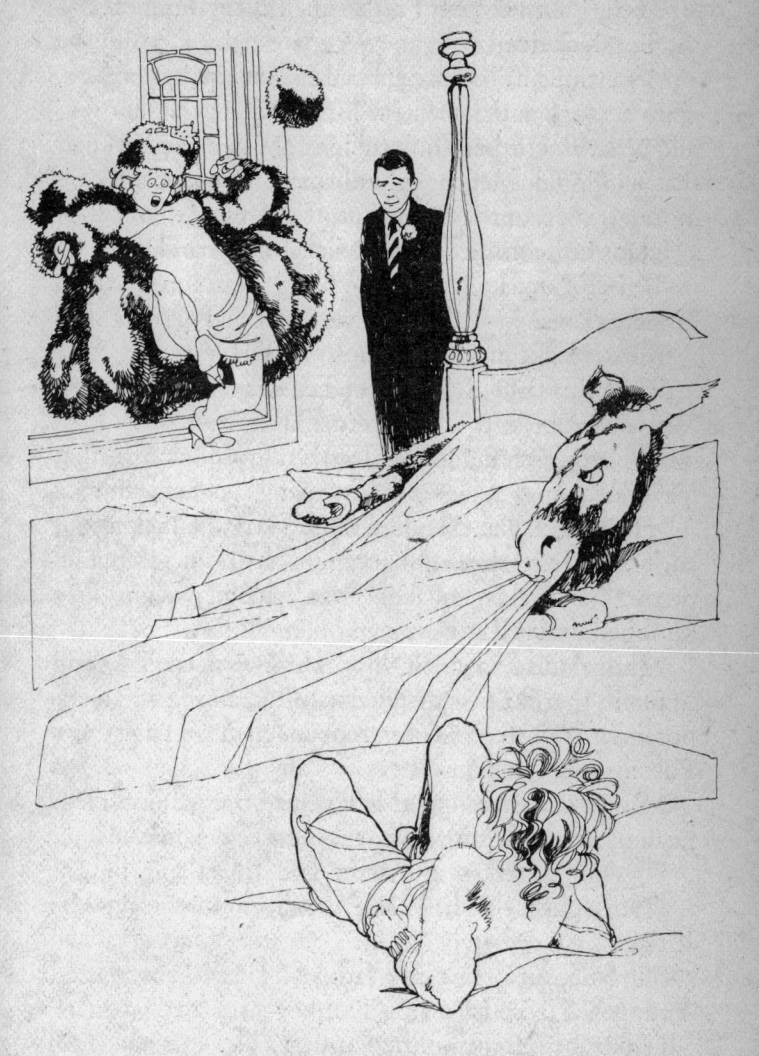

donkey in any colour you like, gold for example, or diamond-studded, it is the very latest thing, you'll be the envy of all your friends, Madam, my goodness, they'll say, I wonder where Mrs Atkins got that!"

"What are the bedknobs made of?" said Mrs Atkins.

"Solid gold, Madam, of course! Perhaps you'd care to try it, Madam? People find the rounded curves of the Donkeyform Bedwarmer very satisfying!"

"I do believe I will!" giggled Mrs Atkins coyly, and leapt into bed with the Donkeyform Bedwarmer.

Rufus woke up with a jolt as Mrs Atkins's new tiara jabbed into the back of his neck. He had been very deeply asleep, and his blurred impression of a lot of fur and teeth made him leap to the conclusion that he was being attacked by a gang of mad minks. Heehawing in a shrill and panicky way, he kicked out all four feet at once. Only one of them made contact with Mrs Atkins, but that was enough to send her flying out of bed towards an open window.

Marmalade had been very deeply asleep too, and thought that she was probably still dreaming when she woke up to the sound of screams and heehaws, and the sight of her mother in four fur coats and a diamond tiara half in and half out of the window, legs waving wildly in an effort to keep her balance.

"Hello, Mum," said Marmalade. "Been shopping?"

The sight of Marmalade was too much for Mrs Atkins.

"Prettiman!" she said sternly, "This is not what I expect of Harrods!"

Then she fell out of the window.

Marmalade Hits the Big Time

Marmalade's mother was wearing so many fur coats when she fell out of the window at Harrods that she only suffered slight injuries when she landed on the fruit barrow six floors below. They took her to hospital, though, to be on the safe side, and she landed up in the next bed to Mr Atkins, who was still recovering from his death-defying dive off Nelson's Column. The whole story made a very amusing little news item on Breakfast Television, and Marmalade and Rufus had a good laugh at it as they lay in bed in the Golden Fleece Suite of the Ritz Hotel, eating their breakfast (oats for Rufus, Rice Krispies for Marmalade).

The next item on TV showed a lot of people in red coats and hard hats making horses jump over high fences.

"Disgustin'!" said Rufus. "It ain't right and it ain't natural."

"But it's the Horse of the Year Show!" said Marmalade. "Can't we go to it? It's in London, at Olympia!"

"Oh, we're going all right," said Rufus grimly. "Firstly, I got us a little job there . . ."

"Really?" said Marmalade. "That's brill!"

"Secondly," said Rufus, "I got a little bone to pick with that feller!" Marmalade looked back at the television. A big swarthy-looking man in riding gear had appeared, towering over the interviewer.

"And here's Buster Creighton, controversial character of the show jumping world," said the interviewer.

"Big headed bully of the show jumping world, more like," grumbled Rufus.

"Tell me, Buster, what's your secret? Will you win again this year?" asked the interviewer eagerly.

"My secret," said Buster Creighton, poking the interviewer hard with his riding crop, "is making 'em do what I want 'em to do—and that goes for people *and* horses!"

"That's what he thinks!" said Rufus, banging the remote control with his hoof. "Come on, young Marmalade, let's get over to Olympia, wherever that is!"

Working backstage at the Horse of the Year Show sounds like a Great Thrill and Really Being In The Big Time, but it depends on what job you're doing. Rufus had a better job than Marmalade. He was working as a Minder again, keeping the big horses company and calming their nerves down. Marmalade watched him mooching about amongst the huge show jumpers, who all treated him with great respect. He didn't seem to do much, but the contrary ones followed him wherever he wanted to go, and the nervous ones stopped jumping about and flashing the whites of their eyes when Rufus nudged and nuzzled them. He really was the best minder in the business, but in a way Marmalade wished he'd get them going instead of calming them down.

Marmalade's job was mucking out. It was a hard job and a smelly one, because, as you might imagine, forty big show jumpers produce quite a lot of muck. But after she'd shifted forty barrowloads of muck, and Rufus had helped to lead the forty big show jumpers back into their clean stalls, it was time for a break. Ten minutes to go before the big show started. Ten minutes before the fanfares and the spotlights and the booming loudspeakers. Ten minutes before the stars of the show jumping world would sweep in wearing their flashy red coats and shiny hard hats, get on their horses, and make them jump over things they didn't want to jump over.

"Like to meet a few of the lads?" said Rufus. He led Marmalade along the line of stalls, where the best horses in Europe hung their patient gloomy handsome heads over the doors, mildly sniffing the air. On each stall was the name of the horse inside, and very peculiar names they had too. There was Cheapo Cheapo Aluminium Double Glazing ("his real name's Graham," said Rufus, "very nice young hoss"). There was a rather haughty-looking black horse with a sheepskin noseband called Schatzenkapper Electronic Dishwasher ("he's Walter," said Rufus, "bit of a

moaner but there ain't no real harm in him at all").
Next there was Viking Low-Calorie Six-Pack Takeaway ("Irish Billy," said Rufus, "used to be the life
and soul of the paddock till they broke his spirit.
How's it going, Billy boy?")

Marmalade felt quite sorry for Irish Billy as he
stood there swinging his head sadly from side to side.

"Why do they give them those daft names?" she
asked.

"Dunno," said Rufus. "Cos they're barmy I 'spect."

Then they came to the last stall. On the door it said:
"Fujiyama 14-day Super Video Recorder with Picture
Search. Owner: Buster Creighton."

"Makes you spit, don't it?" said Rufus. "That's
Arthur, that is. Nicest hoss you could hope to meet.
All right if we come in for a minute, Arthur?"

Arthur stood aside politely as Rufus lifted the latch
with his nose, and they went inside.

"All right, Arthur?" said Rufus.

Arthur snorted and looked doubtfully at Marmalade.

"'S all right," said Rufus. "Marmalade Atkins, mate
of mine. You can talk in front of her."

"Ooh, Rufus," said Arthur. "What a life. Seen what
they're calling me now?"

"Bloomin' disgrace," said Rufus.

"And all the jumping an' that," said Arthur. "Used
to like a bit of a jump, on me own, for fun like, but
that Mr Creighton weighs half a ton, makes me do it
when I'm not in the mood, hits me if I don't, it's a
hard life Rufe."

"Why don't you give him a seeing to?" said Marmalade. "You're bigger than he is."

"Ah, miss, more than me oats is worth," said Arthur. "I used to be a right tearaway, you ask Rufus there, but Mr Creighton's broke me spirit he has."

"Listen," said Rufus. "I got a bit of a plan." But just as he said it, a loud harsh voice rang out just behind them.

"What's all this? Dirty donkeys and scruffy urchins cluttering up the place? Get out of it, the pair of you!"

Marmalade looked up at the fierce swarthy face under the shiny hard hat.

"Who d'you think you are, cock?" she said.

"I'm Bad Buster Creighton, shrimp, and this is the toe of me boot!"

And Bad Buster Creighton kicked Marmalade and Rufus right out of the stall. To Marmalade's amazement Rufus took it like a lamb, and just mooched quietly away, followed by Bad Buster's loud scornful laughter.

"Why didn't you kick him back, Rufus? I was all set to get in there! I was right behind you!"

"Ah," said Rufus mysteriously. "Bidin' me time. Night's not over yet. Besides, I reckon Arthur gets first go. He's a bit low in his spirits just now, but I reckon he's got a bit of a caper left in him, if we gets it right."

"What's the plan, Rufus?" said Marmalade.

But Rufus just winked, and wouldn't say anything else.

Marmalade and Rufus watched the Grand Puissance

Final from the sidelines. Every time one of the horses knocked a fence down, Marmalade and Rufus had to rush out with the other helpers and build it up again. It was hard work, because the fences and walls in the Grand Puissance Final are terrifyingly high and thick, and get higher with every round. Soon all the riders were eliminated except for the very best. Then Cheapo Cheapo Aluminium Double Glazing got careless and kicked a few bricks off the top of the Great Wall, and went off for the early rub-down. "Hard luck, Graham, old cock!" said Marmalade as she ran out to build up the bricks. Next, Viking Low-Calorie Six Pack Takeaway decided he was fed up with the whole business and completely refused to jump over the Horrible Spike-Top Fence.

"Well, why should he?" said Rufus. "Not as if there was anything interesting on the other side."

But Arthur (or Fujiyama Video, as the announcer called him) did everything he was supposed to do, much to Marmalade's disgust, even though the vile Buster Creighton was hitting him with his riding crop, kicking with his heavy boots, cuffing him across the ears, and generally treating him rotten. He sailed across the fences without dislodging so much as a brick or a straw. Soon it was between Arthur and Walter (the Schatzenkapper Electronic Dishwasher) whose rider, a German colonel called Ulrik Schmuck, carried a fearsome duelling sabre, and cursed poor Walter with horrible German oaths.

But in the final jump-off, just as Walter was approaching the Monstrous Mound, someone in the background let out a loud hee-haw (the culprit was never identified), Walter wheeled round to see what was happening, and Colonel Schmuck slipped off sideways and fell right on his sabre. His injuries were not serious, but he was unable to sit down for ten days.

"Ladies and gentlemen," boomed the loudspeakers, "with all the other contestants being eliminated, the supreme champion is Buster Creighton on Fujiyama Video, who will now attempt the World Record Show jump ... the ten foot Giant Haystack! Haystack builders in the ring, please!"

Marmalade and Rufus ran on with the rest of the Haystack builders while Buster Creighton trotted poor old Arthur round the ring, grinning horribly, waving his hat in the air, and giving Victory signs to the crowd. Up went the Giant Haystack piece by piece until it was towering over the sweating builders. There was a narrow gap between two sections. Marmalade was just about to shove a big lump of turf into the space when Rufus caught the scruff of her neck between his teeth, shoved her through the gap, and followed her in. Then the gap closed behind them.

"We're trapped!" gasped Marmalade, spitting out straws.

"All part of the plan, young Marmalade!" said Rufus, who was busy chewing them out a comfortable nest in the middle of the giant Haystack.

It was warm and cosy, if faintly prickly inside the haystack. The roar of the crowd and the booming of the loudspeakers and trombones were muffled, and

Marmalade couldn't see a thing until Rufus neatly nibbled a couple of spyholes. They were going to have a real close-up view of Buster Creighton's world record attempt. It was better than being in the front row.

The huge hall fell silent, silent except for the sound of Arthur's hooves as he trotted round and round the ring, warming up for the great jump. Then a bell rang, and through the spyhole Marmalade saw Arthur cantering straight towards her, with Buster Creighton on his back. She held her breath.

Just as Arthur was about to take off, Rufus stuck his head out of the haystack.

"Hey up, Arthur!" he said, and let out a giant hee-haw.

Arthur stopped dead and stared at Rufus with surprise and pleasure. Buster Creighton didn't stop dead. He sailed over the Giant Haystack on his own, and landed on his bottom on the other side with a thud that shook the foundations. The crowd roared with laughter at the sight of the scruffy ginger donkey with his head sticking out of the haystack rubbing noses with the best showjumping horse in the world, and Buster Creighton drummed his heels on the floor with rage.

"Go on, Arthur," said Marmalade. "Show 'em how easy it is on your own!"

"Right, I will, Miss!" said Arthur, and he trotted back a few paces, then took off and sailed easily over the huge obstacle, nearly landing on Buster Creighton's head. Then he kicked up his heels and did a little dance, and the crowd roared with delight.

Buster Creighton was not delighted. He had been made a fool of by his own horse! Seizing his riding crop, he grabbed furiously at Arthur's reins. But Arthur skipped sideways, and did another little dance as Buster Creighton fell on his face. Arthur was enjoying himself for the first time in years. He trotted bouncily round the outside of the ring, turning his head to grin at the crowd with his huge yellow teeth, and catching the apples and carrots they tossed to him. Every now and then he would slow down to let Buster Creighton catch up, then dance away again as his enraged rider grabbed for the reins. Finally in a last despairing effort, Buster Creighton managed to grab Arthur's tail and hang on. This was not a good idea. Fujiyama 14-Day Super Video Recorder didn't seem to mind a bit. He towed Buster Creighton at high speed through two piles of horse dung, three piles of sawdust, and a holly hedge, and finally galloped out of the ring to the sound of fanfares and frantic applause. He had got his own back on Buster Creighton at last.

When the excited crowds had filed out of Olympia, and the showjumpers were being loaded into their horseboxes, Marmalade and Rufus crept out of their hiding place.

"Ar," said Rufus in a satisfied way. "I knew old Arthur 'ad it in 'im. Just needed bringin' out, that's all!"

"What now?" said Marmalade. "Supper and bed?"

"Not yet awhile," said Rufus. "Got another little job before we goes to bed."

"What's that then?"

"Well," said Rufus. "They booked us to do the cabaret at the Horse of the Year Show Ball."

"Blimey," said Marmalade. "Now we're really in the Big Time!"

And they really were. The Horse of the Year Show Ball was a really posh affair at the Dorchester Hotel, with all the famous horsy people in their best evening dress and hunting pink, and all the ladies looking like mad reindeer with their giant branching tiaras. Marmalade and Rufus got a tremendous reception when they came on. (Rufus wore a huge and dazzling white tie. He explained to the audience that he didn't need tails; he had a perfectly good tail of his own.)

All the routines went down brilliantly. Marmalade sang "The Higher up the Mountain", Rufus gave them his celebrated Solo Donkey Dance Routine, and Arthur came on and did a short guest spot, in which he jumped over ten tables in a row then stood on his hind legs and caught cream buns in his mouth. This was greeted with rapturous applause, and several ladies rushed up and kissed Arthur, which made him feel rather shy, so he went for a lie down at the back of the stage.

Then it was time for Rufus to do his signature tune. His signature tune was called "Good Time Rufus", and Marmalade was impressed to see that he had made up a special chorus for the occasion, which went like this:

They call me Good Time Rufus
And I'm starring in a Big Time Show
They call me Good Time Rufus
And the ladies say I'm all the go!
I've arrived, folks, I'm here,
I'm the Donkey of the Year!
Oh yes I'm Good Time Rufus
And I'm really in the Big time Now!

Holding up their hands to quieten the ecstatic fans, Marmalade and Rufus were just about to go into the encore, when suddenly there was an announcement over the loudspeaker:

"And now, ladies and gentlemen, a surprise mystery guest!"

There was a roll on the drums, and on came Bad Buster Creighton, dressed in a big striped suit like a gangster.

"Ladies and gents," he said. "Just to show there's no bad feelings, and Buster knows how to take a joke, I'd like to do a little song with our friends here!"

"Good old Buster! What a sport!" yelled the audience, and Marmalade thought to herself that Buster Creighton couldn't be such a bad sort after all, if he was ready to let bygones be bygones.

"Just take your lead from me, kid," said Bad Buster Creighton. "Hum along with the tune, and follow my fancy footwork in the soft shoe shuffle. And let me say I'm proud to be on stage with the pair of you!"

"Thanks a lot, cock," said Marmalade.

"Harrumph!" said Rufus.

They got into line, the orchestra struck up the tune, and Buster started to sing:

> They call me Bad Buster Creighton,
> And I'm really aggravatin'
> Got a mad, bad look about me eyes;
> I been warned off all the courses
> Cos I'm bad to all the horses,
> And now Buster's going to give you
> A Nasty Surprise!

Suddenly the orchestra stopped dead, and Buster pulled out a sawn-off shotgun from beneath his striped gangster coat!

"The act's over!" shouted Bad Buster Creighton. "Now for the real thing! All the gold cups, all the jewels, all the tiaras, all the gold rings! Come on, I want 'em all! I'm finished with the lot of you, I'm off to Rio de Janeiro! You'd laugh at the great Buster Creighton, would you? Well now Buster Creighton's got the last laugh!"

There was dead silence. Then the ladies started to take their necklaces and tiaras off, and the men started to gather up the gold cups. Marmalade looked desperately at Rufus, but he was just standing there staring dopily in his white bow tie as if the whole thing was quite beyond him.

Then an amazing thing happened. The curtains parted at the back of the stage, and Arthur the show jumper ambled forward, for all the world as if he were taking a quiet stroll around the stable yard. He stopped just behind Bad Buster Creighton. Marma-

lade held her breath wondering what he would do. So did the audience. But Arthur didn't kick Buster Creighton off the stage. He didn't rear up on his hind legs and stomp Buster Creighton on the head. Slowly and carefully, with a big horsy grin on his face, as if he was doing something he'd been wanting to do for years, he *climbed on Buster Creighton's back*.

Buster Creighton was an immensely strong man. But Arthur the show jumper was a very heavy horse. Buster Creighton staggered and tottered for seven whole seconds. Then he fell flat on his face, with Arthur on top of him, and there was a sound like all the air going out of a punctured football. Then the lights went out.

"Best be off now," said a hoarse voice. "Don't want to outstay our welcome. Just keep close, and follow the smell of Rich Old Donkey."

Five minutes later, Marmalade, Rufus and Arthur were lolling comfortably about in the back of Perkins's little grey horsebox, which was threading its way quietly through the London traffic towards the M1 and the quiet countryside of Warwickshire. Marmalade was chewing bubblegum, Rufus was drinking from a brown bottle, and Arthur was supping a mixture of oats and Guinness from a rather handsome Gold Cup.

"Here, cock," said Marmalade. "Isn't that the Gold Cup for the Horse of the Year?"

"Only fair, innit?" said Rufus. "Won it, didn't he? He *is* the Horse of the Year, ain't you, Arthur?"

Arthur raised his nose from the cup.

"I always wondered," he said, "what it was like to ride on folks' backs."

"I never done it," said Rufus. "What *is* it like?"

Arthur paused to think about it.

"Don't know what folks see in it," he said at last.

There was another long pause. Marmalade felt happy and sleepy. She was going back to Warwickshire, going back to see Torchy and Gypsy and Rover the Free Range Piglet. That felt all right.

"Well, Marmalade Atkins," said Rufus. "We hit the Big Time all right this week. I don't know about you, but I fancies a bit of the Small Time now, meself."

"Right, cock," said Marmalade Atkins.